Illustrations by Artful Doodlers

EGMONT

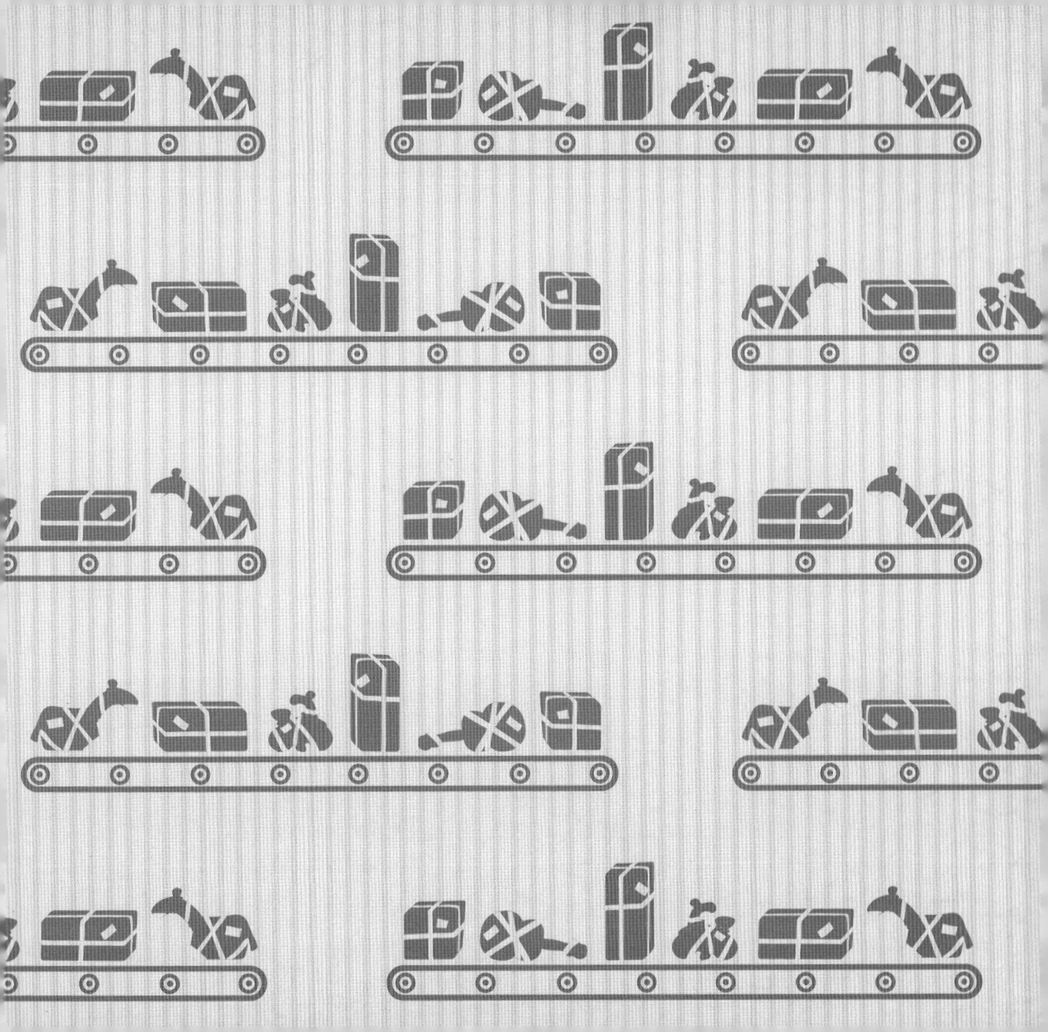

EGMONT

We bring stories to life

First published in Great Britain 2009 by Egmont UK Limited
The Yellow Building,1 Nicholas Road, London W11 4AN

ISBN 978 1 4052 4578 4

46178/5

Printed in Italy

Egmont is passionate about helping to preserve the world's remaining ancient forests. We only use paper from legal and sustainable forest sources.

This book is made from paper certified by the Forest Stewardship Council® (FSC®), an organisation dedicated to promoting responsible management of forest resources. For more information on the FSC, please visit www.fsc.org. To learn more about Egmont's sustainable paper policy, please visit www.egmont.co.uk/ethical

Everyone is surprised when they see Postman Pat's special delivery is a cow! Will Postman Pat be able to prove that no job is too big for the Special Delivery Service?

Postman Pat was delivering Ted's post, when his phone rang its special ring.

"Special Delivery Service, Postman Pat speaking," he answered. There was a loud crash on the other end of the phone.

"Can you get here really quickly?" said Ben at the mail centre, and then the phone went dead.

"Jess, it sounds like Ben needs our help!" said Postman Pat.

PAT4

When Postman Pat got to the mail centre and saw the special delivery he couldn't believe his eyes!

"Meet Daisy, your special delivery for today," announced Ben. "She's for Alf."

The cow licked Postman Pat's face.

"Eugh! Thank you, Daisy. That's enough!" said Postman Pat, edging away.

"The Special Delivery Service can deliver anything," said Postman Pat. "But an animal needs proper care."

"Let's find out what vehicle you'll need," said Ben, tapping on his keyboard.

The computer showed an animal trailer.

"Amy's got a horsebox," said Postman Pat. "I'm sure she'll lend it to us."

Daisy and Jess did not seem to be making friends.

Jess meowed very loudly. The cow mooed and ran out of the mail centre.

"Come back!" called Postman Pat. But the cow was gone!

"I'll go after Daisy!" said Postman Pat. "Ben, you call Amy for help."

The children were at the market, on an outing. They got very excited when they saw Daisy.

"What's a cow doing here?" asked Bill.

"Hey! That's my lunch!" shouted Julian, as Daisy munched his sandwiches.

No one could persuade the cow to move away. Not even PC Selby!

Postman Pat joined PC Selby and the children in the market.

"Please stand back while I catch this special delivery!" Pat said.

He slipped a rope around Daisy's neck, but she ran away, pulling him behind her! Postman Pat couldn't hold on for long, and Daisy charged off out of the town.

"Stop!" called Pat, jumping into his van.

Amy was driving along when she met Daisy in the lane.

"I think I've found your special delivery!" laughed Amy, as Postman Pat drove up.

With a lot of kicking and fussing and mooing, Daisy went into the horsebox.

"Special Delivery Service underway!" cheered a muddy Postman Pat.

But just as she was driving off, Amy heard a strange noise coming from the horsebox.

"That sounds like Jess!" said Amy. "He must have got shut in with Daisy!"

Postman Pat let Jess out and gave him a cuddle. But while they weren't looking, Daisy ambled out and walked away up the cliff path!

Alf drove up on his tractor.

"Alf! Just the man," called Postman Pat. "I've got a special delivery for you. It's a new cow!"

"I can see that!" said Alf. "But what on earth is she doing on that cliff?"

Pat looked up in surprise. Poor Daisy was stuck. She mooed helplessly.

"This is a job for the Special Delivery Service helicopter!" said Postman Pat. "But I'll need Amy's help too."

Postman Pat and Amy rushed back to the mail centre to get the helicopter and the other equipment they needed.

"Operation Rescue Daisy underway!" said Postman Pat, as he took off with Amy hooked on to the winch.

PAT 3

Daisy was very scared by the noise of the helicopter.

"We'd better hurry, Pat," Amy said into her headset.

Postman Pat got the helicopter in position and carefully lowered Amy. She put the harness around Daisy and they were both gently lifted off the ground.

"One special delivery on its way!" said Postman Pat.

No one could believe their eyes when they saw Amy and the flying cow!

Soon they were all safely on the ground, in Alf's field.

"Thank you Amy and Pat," said Alf. "You saved our Daisy!"

"All in a day's work for the Special Delivery Service!" said Postman Pat, as Daisy gave him a big wet kiss. "Mission accomplished!"

PAT 3

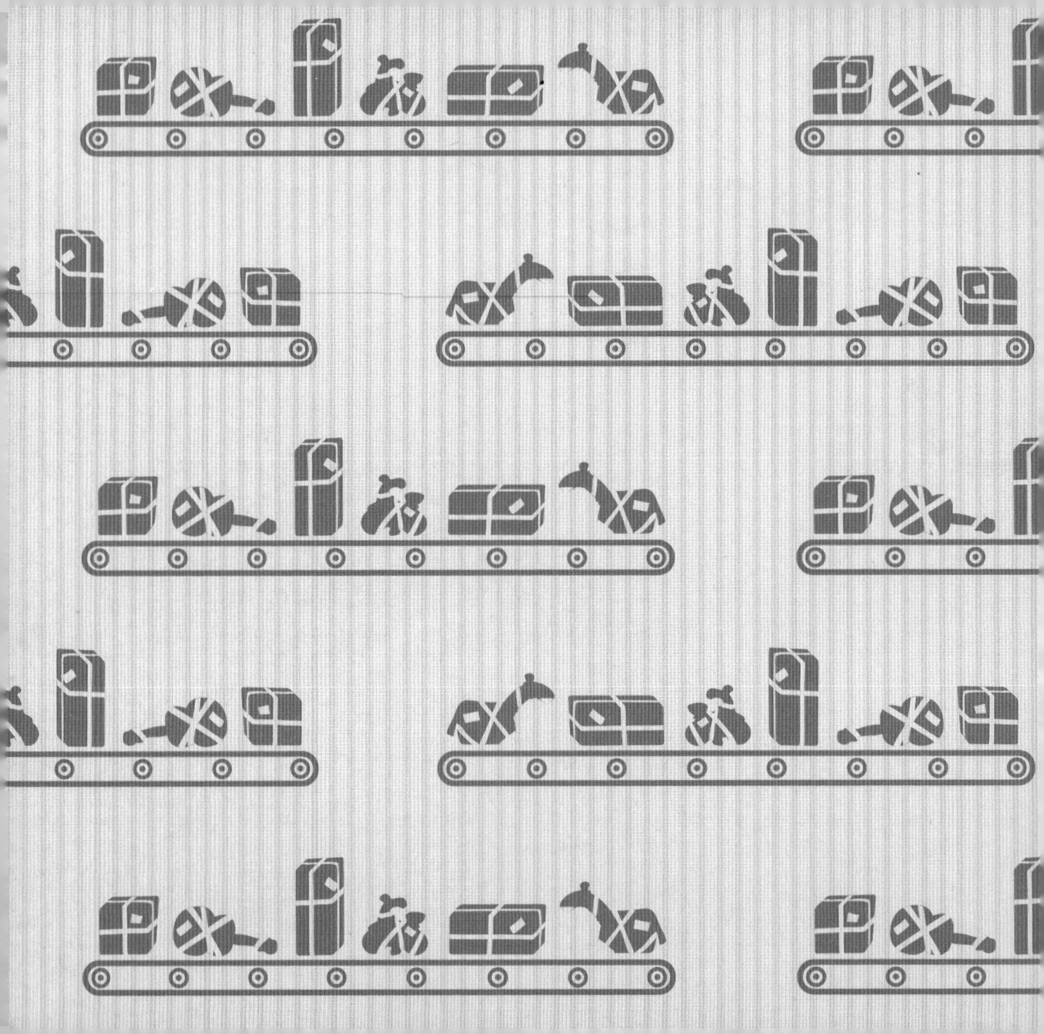